Moonbeam on a cat's ear

Author: Gay, Marie-Louise.
Reading Level: 1.4
Point Value: 0.5
ACCELERATED READER QUIZ# 31619

MOONBEAM
ON A
CAT'S EAR

First published in 1986 by
Stoddart Publishing Co. Limited
34 Lesmill Road
Toronto, Canada
M3B 2T6

Canadian Cataloguing in Publication Data
Gay, Marie-Louise.
    Moonbeam on a cat's ear

ISBN 0-7737-2053-7 (HC)
ISBN 0-7737-5148-3 (QP)

1. Title.

PS8563.A95M66 1986   jC813'.54   C86-093000-9
PZ7.G39Mo 1986

Printed and bound in Hong Kong by
  Scanner Art Services Inc., Toronto

MOONBEAM
ON A
CAT'S EAR

MARIE-LOUISE GAY

For Gabriel

Stoddart

A new moon

shining on a cat's ear.

The cat is dreaming

that a mouse is near.

Knock, knock, knock!

Who's there?

It's Toby Toby

with the bright red hair.

Come on Rosie!

Come out with me!

Let's play in the shadow

of the apple tree.

Now, if I climb real high,

I can pull the moon

right out of the sky.

Shall we sail to Rio, or fly to Mars,

or wander through

the clouds and stars?

Thunder!

And lightning!

Oh Toby Toby, it's so frightening!

Was it a dream

or did they really try

to steal the moon
right out of the sky?